GIFT OF SILENCE

ALFRED SMITH

Published by Water Dragon Publishing
waterdragonpublishing.com

An imprint of Paper Angel Press
paperangelpress.com

ISBN 978-1-957146-87-4 (Trade Paperback)

10 9 8 7 6 5 4 3 2 1

GIFT OF SILENCE

MARA VOSBURG WATCHED STOICALLY as the aspirant's song faded from the air. The plume of fire the young woman had pulled from the ceremonial brazier dissipated as well. The gathered crowd hesitated, and then a chorus of cheers erupted, cascading up into the warm summer air. The other choirmasters seated around her leaned close in whispered discussion, though none sought Mara's opinion.

This young woman's skill was remarkable — especially for a commoner — and, from what Mara overheard of the quiet conferences around her, it wasn't so much *if* she could join a choir, but, rather, which one would get to recruit her. She sighed and leaned back as First Choirmaster Elson rose from his seat and congratulated the young woman while the crowd's cheers grew louder.

The aspirant bowed, flushing, and Mara found herself smiling. There had been few congratulations at her own trial and, with one exception, those had all been grudging. It was nice to see the choirmasters embrace one of common blood so. Elson sat down again, and an expectant hush fell over the crowd.

Mara rose from her bench and bowed respectfully to the First Choirmaster. "It is time for Andinen's trial," she said. "I would ask your leave to stand by him while he proves himself."

"Of course," Elson replied in his rumbling voice. "It would be inappropriate for you to sit in judgment for him. Good luck." As Mara turned away, he added more softly, "I know that his father would have been proud."

Her smiled widened, and she turned to bow again. She then straightened and left the stage, seeking the cordoned area where the remaining aspirants waited. Sweat trickled down the back of her neck, sliding beneath the collar of her heavy ceremonial robe. She wiped it away, cursing the Avalon summer heat.

Why can't they hold the trials in winter? she asked herself, not for the first time. Mara wiped yet more sweat from her face and cast her gaze around the waiting area, looking for her son.

Her eyes settled on Andinen, and her smile slipped for a moment. He was so young. So tiny. As always when she looked at him, she was struck by how much like his father he looked, even now at only five years old. Especially those eyes.

His governess waved and brought Andinen to her. Mara reached out and took his tiny hands in hers.

"Are you ready?" she whispered.

"Yes, Mama," he replied, eyes fixed on the ground.

"Thank Mistress Calwell for watching you."

"Thank you, ma'am," he said. His voice sounded so small.

Mara looked up and nodded to the governess in dismissal, then she rose and turned toward the stairs. By tradition, her son would sing first. Then the next oldest, and so on until all the aspirants had tried. Unlike the woman before, there would be little discussion as to which choir the successful aspirants would join. Most nobles joined the choir of their parents.

She led him up the stairs, helping the short-legged boy climb them one at a time. The rest of the aspirants were older than he by at least eight years, but his instructors had insisted that he was ready.

His father was the same age when he underwent his trial, Mara reminded herself.

Her husband had only had the Vosburg family's reputation to uphold. Now their very place in society rested on Andinen's shoulders.

Mara reached the stage and led Andinen out to stand before the crowd. He looked so tiny standing in front of that massive expanse of people. Most of Avalon City's population stretched out in front of the stage, thousands upon thousands of people waiting to hear her son's voice. He gripped her hand tightly, and she could feel the slight tremble in his little fingers. She squeezed his hand back gently.

He tilted his head up, and Mara met his eyes. She nodded encouragingly, remembering her own trial a decade before. She had barely passed, only able to stir the breeze the smallest amount with her voice. Had Andin Vosburg not been First Choirmaster, she wouldn't have been allowed to join a choir. Wouldn't have been allowed to marry him.

The people of Avalon waited in rapt silence as the boy closed his eyes. His small head tilted to the left, then the right. After five or six heartbeats of focus, he opened his mouth and sang.

A note so clear it could shatter glass sprang from the boy, his beautiful soprano carrying out over the gathered people. The breeze stirred over their heads, the air itself answering Andinen's seeking song.

He changed the timbre of the note, and the breeze gusted with growing force. It swept down upon the stage, and Mara's robes snapped and rippled from its press. Her face split into a wide grin as the note faded. He had done it! He had bent the Unseen Elemental to his will!

Andinen sang a new note, his voice thrumming with power now, and the flames in the brazier surged high. Pride welled in Mara's chest along with the growing fire. He'd so easily shifted between songs, now using his voice to twist a plume of fire into a perfect circle before him.

She waited for the note to fade, for him to start on the next part of the trial. But instead, it grew louder. Grew deeper. She looked down at her son, confused. His voice dropped an octave, then two, until he sang in a resonant bass that rivaled First Choirmaster Elson's.

His voice continued to grow in volume until it was so loud it forced Mara back a step. With the increase in volume, its raw power grew as well. The flames surged higher — far higher than the small brazier should have been able to fuel.

The warm summer air around Mara chilled, then became unbearably cold. The circle of fire spread until it swirled around her and Andinen, a maelstrom of flames lashing upward and blocking the crowd from view.

He's feeding the flames with the warmth of the air.

Over the roar of flames at her back, she was vaguely aware of the choirmasters shouting in alarm. She caught the beginnings of a countersong from the choirmasters, but they were too late. She shivered and clutched her arms, frost crystallizing on her robes. The song grew in volume again, and the flames climbed higher.

Mara lowered herself into the trance-like state of attunement, then shrieked in agony when a searing pain lanced through her skull. Andinen's note warped the space around it, warped the very songs of air and flame he had been singing. It smashed her out of attunement, and she slumped to her knees.

She tried to force her way back into the trance again, but the pain drove through her once more. That terrible voice coming from her son's mouth shifted down yet another octave, and she felt rather than heard it. It was so deep the bones rattled in her chest. Mara sunk to her knees with her hands clutched to her ears, sobbing in agony.

One last time she tried, but this time the pain overwhelmed her. Her eyes fluttered, and she fell forward onto her face. The last image seared into her mind was that of her son, hands outstretched and still singing. She tried to cry out, to beg him to stop, and then merciful darkness took her.

•　　•　　•

Andinen. Mara's mind slipped back to consciousness. *Andinen needs help.*

She drew in a deep, shuddering breath and gagged on air thick with smoke. Her eyes crept open, and her coughing trailed off into stunned silence. Festival Square of Avalon was in ruins; the only movement was drifts of fine ash stirred by a gentle breeze.

She should be burned to a cinder like everything around her. She slid her hands down her body, checking for pain. Nothing but some minor singeing. Mara turned her gaze up then, out toward the rest of the city. The sight made her gasp, starting another coughing fit.

Plumes of smoke curled from husks that had once been proud marble towers — monuments to the greatest harmonizers who had ever lived. The immaculately manicured gardens of Festival Square were now reduced to naught but piles of char and ash. Here and there a foot or a hand with nothing attached to it poked out from the mounded detritus. All of this devastation wrought from a single song. Her son's song.

She looked down at the ash before her feet. There was no way he could have survived. And yet, she stood there mostly unscathed.

I need to find him. Comfort him. He'll be so scared.

The thought rattled around her numb mind, incongruous with the scene of ruin around her.

A shout from nearby snapped her from her reverie. Figures wearing the uniform of the choirguard emerged from a street that led off from Festival Square. She raised a hand and tried to speak, but all that came out was a dried croak. Her throat was seared, parched. Mara tried to clear it to no avail.

Still feeling numb, she walked to the edge of the square on shaky legs, wiping some of the grime from her face with the heavy sleeve of her robe. The garment was ruined anyway. Fine Suldenese silk, now worthless. She almost laughed at the absurdity of her concern.

The whole central district is in ruins, and you're worried about your clothing?

The incongruous amusement cracked the dam keeping her emotions in check, and panic swiftly followed. Her heart crashed into her stomach, and the dam broke.

He's still alive, she realized. He had to be. If she was still unscathed, then wouldn't he have made it out as well?

She sucked down another lungful of smoky air and hunched over as another coughing fit racked her body. This, at least, got the attention of the choirguard. They rushed over and surrounded her, the leader stepping forward and grabbing her shoulder.

"Lady Mara?"

She knew that voice. Festin. A young captain who had been given the hardship duty of guarding the widow of Andin Vosburg. Of looking after her. Despite the snub implied in the post, he attended to it with a faithfulness almost verging on worship.

"Festin," she managed to croak between coughs, letting him straighten her up. "Festin, where is he? Please tell me you found him!"

"Found who, Lady Mara?" A hint of worry crept into Festin's voice. "Please. You must come with us. Choirmaster Vel is organizing the rescue efforts. She's asked that any ranking harmonizers be brought to her to assist." His hand slid down to grip her arm, pulling her away.

"Forget Vel," Mara replied. Now that she'd spoken a few words, her voice grew more firm with every syllable. "You need to help me find Andinen. He's still alive."

"Can't be," Festin replied, tightening his grip on her shoulder and leading her away from the square. "Nobody could have survived that ..." He trailed off.

"I'm still here," Mara said. "Please. He's alive. He must be alive." The panic crashed against her once more. She *had* to find him. Her son was all she had in this life. Ever since Andin had died.

"Let me take you to Vel," Festin said more firmly, pulling her by the shoulder while the rest of the guardsmen formed a protective circle around them. "We'll see what she has to say."

Mara tried to pull away, but Festin held her close. "Lady Mara," he said with surprising firmness. "We can better search for Andinen with the help of the remaining choirmasters."

The logic of his statement hit home, and the panic driving her lost its momentum. In its place, exhaustion poured through her. It seeped into her muscles, and she sagged against Festin, burying her face in the shoulder of his azure uniform and letting the tears come. He guided her steps, leading her.

An errant breeze stirred the air, and the overwhelming scent of burning was replaced by something else. Mara gagged and retched at the smell of pork left too long in the sun and then charred to a crisp.

People, she realized.

She pulled her face from Festin's shoulder and looked around. They were leaving Festival Square, heading to places where the flames hadn't fully consumed the bodies they'd touched. She closed her eyes and breathed through her mouth, fighting the urge to vomit before opening them again.

More people bustled around here, some wearing the azure of the choirguard, others wearing the garb of commoners. There were precious few wearing the formal robes of the harmonizers.

Mara's stomach dropped. *We were all in Festival Square. Almost every choirmaster and most of the harmonizers in the city.*

All around her choirguard and commoner alike dug and sifted through the charred remains of buildings. Mara's gorge rose again, but she forced it down. She drew herself up tall and set her face. She was, after all, a harmonizer. Even if she was among the least powerful in the city.

"Where was Vel that she survived? Where were you, for that matter?" Mara asked, looking Festin up and down.

His always immaculate uniform was stained by soot and torn in several places. Half the hair atop his head had been burned away to leave an angry red scalp beneath.

"I was standing in a doorway when the blast hit. Got lucky. Vel's choir came late, in protest of the unblooded aspirants. Didn't even come to hear the sponsored. They were at the back of the crowd when" — he glanced at Mara, discomfort plastered across his face — "when it happened."

"Purists," Mara muttered with a shake of her head.

Her stomach clenched again. If Vel and her cadre were the primary survivors, that meant …

She fought the thoughts down. *Find Andinen. Deal with politics later.*

What few people were in the street gave way before her and her escort, the common folk nodding deferentially to Mara.

She followed Festin away from the square, toward areas less devasted by the out-of-control song. Still, the scene was horrifying. They were far enough away now that the song of fire had faded and left some survivors in its wake. Some still cried for help from beneath collapsed buildings, their voices hoarse from long hours inhaling smoke. Others simply screamed wordless sounds of pain that raked at Mara's heart.

Some streets had been spared the flame entirely, but had not been left unscathed. For a stretch, the cobbles were rent apart in a great crevasse that swallowed up the sun's light before it could illuminate the bottom. She followed Festin and his squadron around it, glancing nervously at the buildings teetering on the edge of the great pit. Like it was some ancient beast yearning to swallow them up. Mara shuddered, and Festin quickened his pace. The pit seemed to make him uneasy as well.

Festin led her to another square, smaller than the festival's, but clear of rubble and char. At long last, she saw other figures wearing robes that matched hers. A few dozen. That was all. They stood beneath a tent, all speaking at once, so their voices blended together into a general hum of sound. Festin approached and saluted sharply.

"Choirmaster Vel," he said, giving a half bow in deference. "I've found Lady Vosburg."

Vel's head snapped up, and she leveled a glare at Mara. "You survived? Out of all the choirmasters?" The last came with a twist of the lips.

Despite her exhaustion, Mara flushed with anger. Vel and her ilk thought that she only held her title out of deference to her dead husband. It hurt even more that they weren't entirely wrong.

Mara knew she had barely passed the tests to join a choir, let alone achieve the rank of master. Andin's death had forced her into the role despite her lack of ability, his family being able to trace their lineage back to the founding of Avalon. That shame would do no good right now.

"Please," she said, pushing past the ring of harmonizers to stand directly in front of Vel. "My son is alive. We need to find him."

"We have more important things to take care of right now," Vel said with a sneer. "We don't have time to look for the murderer. Even if he did survive."

Mara recoiled as though struck. "Murderer? He. Is. A. Child." She bit off each word and thrust her finger at Vel.

"Choirguard Captain Festin, remove Lady Vosburg. She is clearly overwrought from the loss of her child."

"Choirmaster," Festin said, "I think it's worth hearing her —"

"I said remove her. Now."

Festin bowed his head. "Yes, Choirmaster." He placed a gentle hand on Mara's shoulder and guided her away. "I'll see Lady Vosburg back to her estate."

"Very good," Vel replied. "Leave your squadron with me. I have other uses for them."

"He's alive!" Mara said, desperation tingeing her voice. Festin pulled her away. "He's alive!" Mara was screaming now.

She tried to struggle against his grip, but the fight left her body once again. Exhaustion rolled over her like a wave crashing onto a shore, and Festin led her from the square and around a corner. Mara pulled from his grip and slumped against a wall.

Her tears came uncontrolled now, and her knees went weak. She slid to the dirty street, arms wrapping around her knees. She repeated those words like a mantra over and over.

"He's alive. He's alive. He's alive."

A hand rested on her shoulder, and Festin knelt before her.

"I believe you," he said.

She blinked, tears streaming through the ash smudging her face.

"I believe you," he repeated. "If you survived, then Andinen could have as well."

He rose and looked back the way they had come. Something warred behind his eyes for a moment, and then his expression firmed.

"It's my duty to help you find him. Let's go."

Mara looked up at him, into eyes that gazed at her with unending compassion and faith. Maybe even something approaching love.

Hope flared to life in her chest, and she rose. "Thank you," she whispered. Her eyes drifted up toward the waning sun. "I think I know how to find him."

She closed her eyes and drew in a deep breath, the air here clear enough that she didn't cough. Mara let that breath out slowly, lowering herself into the trance of attunement, blocking out ambient noise so she could listen for the song of the Unseen Elemental. She found that void, and then pain lanced through her mind. A cacophonous flood of discordant notes pounded through her thoughts. Wind pulled from its natural course, flames bent to the will of a mortal. Even the earth itself cried out, having been torn asunder by some terrible force. The assault of sound shattered her attunement and left her clutching her ears in shock.

"What's wrong?" Festin's voice sounded far away, and she blinked her vision clear, looking up at him. "Are you all right?" he asked.

Mara nodded, normal hearing restored. She paused a moment before speaking. "There's something amiss with the Unseen Elemental."

Festin nodded. "Vel said something about that. Explaining why they weren't using harmonizing to clear the rubble and put out the fires."

"This shouldn't be possible." Mara closed her eyes again. "I just need to listen for a moment."

She fell into attunement once more. This time, she was ready for the hellish cascading song that assaulted her mind, and she gritted her teeth against the pain. She had to listen for Andinen.

There!

Just as the pain grew too great, she caught the faint echo of a small song in the distance. Then her attunement shattered, and she was again left clutching her ears.

"That way," she said, pointing vaguely east. "He's that way. I heard him."

She strode off down the street, farther away from the most devasted part of the city. Purpose reenergized her aching, exhausted limbs, and soon she was all but running.

The streets here were almost entirely empty, their inhabitants likely helping with rescue efforts. Mara lost track of how many blocks she ran, but when she finally slowed, her breath came in ragged gasps. The odor of charred flesh had been left behind, and she gratefully sucked down the clean air.

It came from this direction.

She closed her eyes once more and let herself settle into attunement again.

Though the chaotic symphony was weaker, it was still there. The rumbling of stone split apart by unchecked power. The thrum of flame stirred to destruction by a song that had slipped the shackles of a harmonizer's voice.

This time she managed to force it out. She found the void of attunement. That absolute silence that was required for harmonizing. Once there, she began to listen. Her tutors had told her it was like standing in a dark room with unlit candles.

Light them with care, let the light creep back in. Open your mind little by little. Let the music of the Unseen Elemental drift back till you hear the song you're looking for.

It was difficult to pick out another harmonizer's song when they were singing themselves. It was supposed to be impossible when they weren't actively singing. For Mara, Andinen was a special case. She'd known that song since she'd first held him as an infant, and she could pick him out of a crowd. Could track him for miles.

Mara let the ambient sound of the world back in little by little, as though lighting those candles one at a time. She heard the waning thrum of the sun's fire as it lost its battle against the horizon. Likewise, she heard the swell of the Cortus River as it made its languid way around the city. Then, barely audible, she caught Andinen's song once more. Her heart twisted in her chest, and she almost lost her attunement. She heard the song of his tears, familiar to her on a primal level. She'd heard it when she'd first clutched him to her breast to nurse. She knew where he was.

Her attunement faded away, and without waiting for Festin, she followed the trail. By now the streets seemed almost normal, so far removed from the devastating blast. The faces of well-appointed town houses stared down at her, the setting sun glinting in their windows. She held her breath as she walked, pausing after every step to listen.

Then she heard what she so desperately wanted. Soft sobs coming from an alley. A child's sobs. She stepped between the brick buildings, and there, in the darkness, found a huddled figure.

"Andinen?" Mara called. She received a sob in reply. She repeated his name, drawing closer. This time, a soot-stained face with pale blue eyes rimmed red from crying looked up at her.

"Mama?" he said, sobbing. The five-year-old lurched into her outstretched arms. He babbled at her through his tears; the only word she picked out was "Mama," again and again. His tiny hands clung to her arms, soft fingernails digging into her skin with surprising strength.

"Shh, my baby," Mara whispered, running her fingers through his deep brown hair covered in grime. "Shh, my baby."

The boy sobbed into her shoulder. "I didn't want to. I didn't want to hurt anybody. It made me."

It? Mara wondered. She dismissed the notion, simply relieved to have him in her arms. "I've got you," she said to him. She held him close, feeling tears burning her eyes and streaming down her face again. He trembled against her, and Mara began to sing. Not harmonizing. Just a simple lullaby she remembered her grandmother singing to her. One she'd sung to him when he'd been just a baby.

Be still, for night falls,
But fear not, my sweet.
The Lotveddi will keep you
From dangers most deep.
Against monsters and beast
They fight, spears in hand,
To keep your mind safe
And protect our land ...

There were other verses, but that was all she remembered. Her grandmother had been from the far west and said her own mother had taught it to her. She could trace her blood all the way back to the savage Dibarach who lived in those far mountains.

She sang, and his sobbing slowed. She sang, running her fingers through his hair and rocking him gently as his breathing steadied. Still she sang, repeating the single verse over and over again. Finally, she fell silent with Andinen still in her grasp, his chest rising and falling in the rhythmic breathing of sleep.

With care she rose, cradling her son in her arms. The sun had long since surrendered to the night, but the gaslights had yet to be lit. She walked onto a street lit by starlight and little else.

Festin was there, and a smile split his shadowed face. "Thank the gods he's okay," he breathed. "We should tell the others —" His words cut off at a glare from Mara.

"And let them take him?" she snarled, unexpected rage welling up in her chest. "Vel won't let this go."

Festin rocked back on his heels, eyes going wide. "He's just a child."

"Do you think Vel will care? No. Speak of this to no one." She drew a deep breath, struggling to keep the panic from her words. Festin met her eye, and in a soft voice she added, "Please?"

Festin nodded and reached to take Andinen from her, but Mara turned her shoulders away. This was her burden to carry. Hers to care for. She wasn't letting him out of her sight again if she could help it. His angelic face, stained with ash and soot, relaxed into a calm smile. She set herself, and with Festin in tow, carried him home.

•   •   •

Mara hummed the lullaby softly while cradling Andinen's head in her lap. Three days had passed since the festival. Three days since her son had burned the city's center to cinders. That whole time her son had done little but sleep. She had done little but sit with him.

A rhythmic tapping reached her ears, echoing down the hallway. She looked up to see her butler, Milen, standing in the doorway. He held his ivory-tipped cane in one hand and a serving tray in the other.

"Lady Mara, it is time for the young master's dinner." His voice rustled like shifting sheaves of ancient parchment, and he shuffled forward into the nursery.

The tip of his cane gave a muted click with each step on the polished stone floor. He set the platter down on the bedside table and stood, unease plastered across his face. Of all the family attendants, only he had refused the offer of a year's pay in exchange for their silence and dismissal. He and Festin, of course.

Mara rose to take it from him, but Milen gently took her arm. "Please, my lady," he said. "Let me. You need rest and a meal yourself. I've taken the liberty of preparing something in the dining room."

"I —" Mara caught a glimpse of herself in the mirror above the dresser. She looked a mess. Dark hair steadily working its way free from a utilitarian bun. Rumpled clothing. Eyes hollow and lined with worry. When was the last time she'd eaten? Yesterday? Two days ago? Her stomach rumbled at the thought of food, and her protest died on her lips. "Thank you, Milen."

She walked to the doorway, glancing over her shoulder as the butler stirred her son awake. Milen looked at her and nodded toward the door. "Go, Lady Mara. I can look after him while you take care of yourself."

Mara turned away and moved out of the room to the foyer's landing. Milen was right. She needed to look to herself, at least for a little while. Her hand rested on an ornate banister, its heavy bronze kept buffed to a shimmer. She slid her hand along the cool metal as she walked down to the foyer. Not a speck of dust anywhere, with a floor of black marble so polished she could see her reflection in it.

It was nothing but opulence maintained for its own sake. When Andin had been alive, they'd hosted parties for Avalon City's elite. They had come for him, to eat his food and rub shoulders with the others of society's upper crust. And to look down their noses at Mara. None were bold enough to say it to her face while her husband's name protected her, but they had made it clear she didn't belong.

They were right, of course. Mara *was* an outsider in this place: a miller's daughter with naught but a sweet voice and a sharp mind. The gulf between her and Andin's stations hadn't been enough to stop him from falling in love with her, and he had provided for her education in harmonizing so they could marry. Even with the best tutors money could hire, her song was laughably weak.

Numb to the decadent decorations around her, she entered the dining room. The vast mahogany table could easily fit three dozen people, and the single setting laid for her looked small on the polished wood. She pulled out a chair and sat, picking up her cutlery and beginning the meal.

Mara didn't taste the food as she chewed it, mechanically raising fork from plate to mouth again and again. She lost track of time, as she often had these last few days, her mind wandering back to the destruction left in the wake of her son's song. As well as to Festin's accounts of the choirmaster's meetings he attended as her proxy while she recovered from the ordeal.

Another bite. Another swallow. Even when he'd stirred, Andinen hadn't been the same. There was a distance to his gaze that went beyond simple disorientation, and she could have sworn she saw something lurking in the depths of his crystal-blue eyes. Something dark and dangerous. Something that could, perhaps, devastate a city when a mere child should not be able to. She shook her head, dismissing it as fearful fancy. There had to be another explanation.

The front doors flew open, the echoing boom giving way to a single pair of booted feet striking the floor. Festin strode into the foyer, looking around wildly.

She rose from her seat and he met her eye, sprinting toward her. His breathing came in ragged gasps as though he'd run the whole way to her home.

"Lady Mara," he wheezed, "they know about Andinen. They're coming for him."

Mara stood up so quickly her chair toppled over behind her. "Who? When?"

"One of your former servants must have realized he survived. Vel is coming with a contingent of choirguard. She means to try him for the murder of First Choirmaster Elson."

"She can't! He's only a child!"

"They also plan to arrest you," Festin continued, moving back toward the foyer. "She intends to hold you responsible for the destruction he caused."

Mara gathered her skirts and sprinted for the hall. Milen, no doubt responding to Festin's arrival, stood at the top of the stairs.

"What is it, my lady?" he said, his rasping voice only just audible.

"Bar the door!" she shouted up to him, reaching the stairs and taking them two at a time. "Festin, help him."

"Yes, Lady Mara." She heard the sound of the door slamming shut and looked over her shoulder.

"Doubt that will hold them for long," Festin said, drawing a sword in one hand and a dagger in the other.

The guard wore their thin-bladed rapiers and parrying daggers more for show than for function, but Festin was one of the few who kept on his training. The choirguard itself was almost superfluous. Who needed a swordsman as a guard when gouts of flame were but a moment away?

Mara reached the top of the steps, slippered feet slapping against the polished floor. She skidded to a halt in the doorway to the nursery. Her son sat on the bed, looking toward her with vacant eyes.

"Mama?" he said, his voice lacking inflection.

Before she could reply, she heard fists pounding on the door. Then a series of dull thuds. *They're battering down the door.* "Mama, can you hear the song?" Andinen said, sliding from the bed and walking toward her. His movements were stiff. Jerky. Unnatural.

Mara's guts wrenched as a half-dozen notes twined together outside. Vel hadn't just come with the choirguard, she'd brought other harmonizers as well. The foundations of the manor rumbled, and then a splintering sound echoed through the hallway. She closed her eyes and lowered herself into attunement. She wasn't the most powerful, but she could at least do something to protect her son.

The void filled her mind, and she opened it just a crack to listen for the warmth in the air around them. The thrum of flame mixed with the whistle of air filtered through, and then a potent note bullied its way into her mind. Coming from behind her. She opened her eyes and turned. The sound rang from Andinen's mouth. A horrible, twisted song that warped the very air around him.

"Everything will be all right, Mama," her son said, his voice still an emotionless monotone. "We can protect you." Mara watched, stunned, as he walked past her. His body twitched and jerked as he walked, as though not fully in control of his movements. She tried to grab him, but he lurched aside and into the hallway. He headed for the stairs down to the foyer.

Mara forced herself back into attunement, listening again for the warmth in the air around her. If she could keep that heat from the other harmonizers, their songs to fire would be that much less potent. The heat, after all, had to come from somewhere.

She followed Andinen out onto the balcony, ready to call the heat to herself. She nearly lost her focus again when she saw the scene below. Milen lay in a twisted heap by the remains of the door, blood pooling around him. Festin was still standing, vigilant at the foot of the stairs, though one leg had been pierced by a splintered shard of wood.

Two dozen azure uniforms formed a semicircle around him, and behind them stood six harmonizers in their ceremonial robes, with Herati Vel a seventh illuminated in the doorway behind them. Even from a distance, Mara could see Vel's face curl into a cruel smile when her eyes fell on Andinen. She spoke then, her voice ringing through the quiet foyer with a crystalline clarity.

"We have come for the mongrel responsible for the murder of First Choirmaster Elson and countless others," she shouted.

Rage flared in Mara's stomach, and she picked out the note from the flame of the lamps lining the hallway. She called to that fire, her weak song drawing the flickering heat toward her. She'd always lacked the raw power of other harmonizers. It had forced her to hone her control until she was almost without peer — not that it made any difference to the rest of them.

Faster than her foes could react, Mara shifted the timbre of her song. She compressed the flame before her and sent it streaking toward Vel. A small piece of flame, true, but finely controlled and hot as a forge fire. Bad luck caused another harmonizer to shift into its path. The white-hot needle pierced his eye, and he fell to the ground, clutching his face and gurgling wordlessly.

The hallway was plunged into shadow as the lamps flickered out, and Mara again reached for a source of warmth, the lamps at the base of the stair. Now they were ready for her. One of the other harmonizers sang out to counter, his note to the wind battering hers aside with contemptuous ease. His song slammed into her and sent her whirling to the ground.

Again the foyer fell silent, the other harmonizer's note fading from hearing. Again Vel's voice rang out, imperious and demanding. "You would add murder by your own hand to the list of crimes laid at your feet?"

Mara struggled to her feet, spitting out blood from where she'd bitten her tongue. "You can't have him!" she shrieked, a wave of dizziness driving her back to her hands and knees. In the back of her mind, a small part of her recoiled in horror. She *had* just murdered a man. Snuffed his life with little more effort than it took to light a candle.

No time for that. I need to protect Andinen.

Below, Vel issued orders to the choirguard and her retinue. "I want the child alive, if possible. The others don't matter."

Festin screamed in defiance, lunging toward the nearest guardsman arrayed against him. His rapier sank deep, slipping through his foe's sluggish defenses. He withdrew it and stabbed another.

He was a whirlwind of blades, parrying their awkward thrusts and counterattacking. A third fell back, clutching his chest, then a fourth with a hole in his throat. Were they all he had to contend with, Mara thought he might have carried the day, but the choirguard wasn't the only foe arrayed against them.

Vel and the other harmonizers sang, the rumbling in the foundations of the mansion starting anew. Mara forced herself back into attunement and staggered to her feet. She sang a counter harmony in a desperate attempt to block the attack she knew was coming against Festin. And then a powerful song burst forth behind her. Andinen was singing. Not his sharp, clear soprano. No. This was a deep and potent bass that rumbled through Mara's chest and made her very bones buzz.

Vel and her retinue's voices cut off in gurgled shrieks as Andinen's song pushed the warmth from the air. Mara watched in muted shock as frost crystallized on the uniforms of the choirguard below. Then on the harmonizers. Then finally on Vel. The choirmaster turned to run, but her foot froze fast to the ground, and she toppled to the floor.

Festin turned toward Mara, his face contorted in pain and terror. He reached a hand up toward her. His eyes clear for a moment, his expression fearful and pleading. They clouded over with frost, the life fading from them. Finally, he went still. An icy statue frozen in exquisite agony. Still, Andinen sang. He sang until the men and women in the foyer had skin so frozen it looked the color of the night sky.

That cold seared Mara as well, making her lungs burn with every breath. "Andinen," she managed to gasp. "Andinen. Stop, please."

In that terrible moment, he turned his eyes upon her, and Mara screamed. His crystal-blue eyes had vanished, swallowed up by onyx sclera that bled outward until there was nothing but a beckoning darkness. Then he *smiled*. Or at least his lips curled up in a rictus grin. *This is not Andinen.* The last thing she heard was *something* beneath that deep voice. Something ancient. Terrifying. Utterly inhuman. She contorted inward on herself, shivering and spasming. Somewhere behind her the note stopped, and silence fell. Terrible, complete silence.

She was vaguely aware of Andinen walking away from her, toward the nursery. Her clothing was stiff with frost, and she struggled to draw breath. Each time her chest rose and fell, agony shot through her. Her lungs had been seared by the cold.

She pushed herself to her knees and then stood on trembling legs. Every step rubbed stiff clothing against numb skin. A glance down into the foyer told her that there could be no survivors. Better than two dozen statues of men and women stood, crystals of ice dangling. Festin ... Festin was among them. He'd stood by her, stood by her son. And now he was dead by Andinen's hand. She blinked back tears and limped down the shadowy hallway, toward the nursery.

Her son sat on the bed, eyes still fully black. "You live," he said in a rumbling voice that she *felt* in her chest rather than heard. "My vessel asked that you be spared. I will indulge it for now."

"What, what are you?" Mara gasped, each breath still a burning agony in her throat and lungs.

"That is not your concern. Simply serve my vessel as you have been. Continue your work, and you will continue to be spared."

Mara's lips moved in silent shock, and she watched as the darkness bled from Andinen's eyes, returning them to their crystal blue. He blinked. For a moment, she could almost believe she'd imagined the whole thing. That her son was still before her.

"Mama?" he asked, wiping his nose. "Mama, are you all right?"

"I'm fine, Andinen," Mara replied with a shaking voice. "Are you thirsty?"

Her son nodded, and she searched his eyes for any indication of the thing lurking within. She saw nothing.

"Let me get you something to drink."

She turned and limped from the room, her leg protesting with every step. She didn't want to go back to the foyer, back to where those frozen corpses still stood. But she had to.

The railing was icy, as were the steps, and she took them one at a time. Left foot, right foot, next step. She looked over her shoulder, back toward Andinen's room, then down at the bodies still posed in their final agonizing moments. She reached the last steps and tentatively moved into the foyer proper.

Her foot went out from under her on the icy floor, and she grabbed a frozen figure to steady herself. She recoiled in horror and fell to the ground as the form toppled, the legs snapping off at the ankles. Mara shrieked as the body — *Festin's* body — crashed to the ground, shattering into dozens of frozen chunks no bigger than her fist. Mara rolled to the side and vomited, the only meal she'd eaten for over a day spewing across the ground.

Setting her jaw against the pain racking her whole body, Mara rose once more. A plan began to form in her mind. A desperate one, but all she had now was desperation. That *thing* had a voice. It emerged when threatened. She straightened her back and made her way toward the kitchen, taking step after careful step to avoid falling once more.

She reached the kitchen and found what she sought. A pitcher of milk, still fresh from the morning's delivery, sat on the table. Mara took a cup and poured, then added a cube of sugar. She walked to the washbasin and opened the cupboard above it. Inside, nestled behind the soaps and rags, sat two small vials of glass: one black, the other clear. A powerful sleeping draft they'd given to Andin to ease his pain at the end when the sickness grew too great. Two drops had been enough to still his body and mind. The "gift of silence," they called it.

The other vial was an antidote — the gift was basically a poison, after all — to be administered if they gave him too much. She slipped that into the pocket of her dress. The other, she opened.

Mara put a drop from the dark vial into the milk and then froze.

I can't do this.

The risk was too great. She shook her head.

I must do this.

She set her shoulders and let five more drops fall into the mug. She added another bit of sugar, then added five more drops to be sure. She stirred it, humming softly to herself as she did so. Her hands trembled for a moment.

Cup in hand, she headed back to Andinen's room. Another walk through the bodies posed like statues stiffened her resolve. She handed it to him, and he took the drink in both hands.

He looked up at her, eyes still clear of corruption. "Please make the song stop, Mama."

His voice sounded so frail, so tiny. Mara suppressed a sob.

"Shush now, just drink. It'll be all right. I've got you."

He lifted the glass to his lips and took a long swallow. Mara sat next to him on the bed, putting her arms around him and singing again. The same lullaby. She sang it as tears streamed down her face. Andinen's form relaxed in her arms, going still. Then his eyes snapped open, the sclera and pupils filled with an inky blackness. His mouth opened, and a dark mist poured forth.

A tendril of it whipped toward her, and though she tried to dodge away, it pierced her forehead. Pain and terror drove the aches and burns from her thoughts as a searing sensation shot through her mind. The pain faded, and she felt something *prying* at her mind. Seeking to gain purchase.

Where before it had used Andinen's own mouth to communicate, she now felt sensations. Emotions. Concepts. It wanted *in*. Mara slipped into attunement, seeking the calm safety of the trance. The darkness enveloped her, and she clenched her jaw. On the outside of that void, *something* raged.

A very real physical pressure continued to press on her mind. A terrible song that twisted and writhed struggled to burrow inside. Through the barrier in her mind, she felt anger, desire, and a presence older than the song of the earth itself. The song screeched, and she felt its desperation. It pounded on the bastion of her mind, and yet her control persevered.

It had a *song*. It could be controlled.

She fought against the mental invasion, pushing back but letting just the faintest trickle of the thing's song reach her. In a moment, she had the note firmly in her head.

Once she had it, she pushed that trickle from her mind once again. It couldn't be allowed to stay for long. She sang. The note terrible and beautiful all at once. A sound no human voice wanted to make. The timbre of her song drew *it* toward her. She opened her eyes, still singing, and watched it leach from Andinen's still form.

It continued to rail against her mind, struggling to find purchase. She shifted her timbre, pushing it away. Away from her. Away from Andinen. The sound tore at her throat, but she persisted. Pushing it until, just as the pain grew too great, the struggling sensation vanished.

The black miasma hovering above Andinen whirled away from him, its hold on her mind broken. With her last gasp of breath, she held the note for a heartbeat more. The roiling thrashed and spasmed, and then vanished through the wall.

Mara sucked in a desperate breath, coughing as her raw throat protested what she'd done. Her whole body felt wrung out. She wanted nothing more than to simply collapse. But no. *Need to save Andinen.* Her eyes fell to where he lay, head in her lap.

Andinen's breathing came in shallow gasps. Her fingers fumbled the other bottle from her pocket, dropping the delicate crystal stopper to the ground where it shattered into thousands of tinkling pieces. Her free hand pinched his cheeks, forcing his mouth open. She poured the substance down his throat, praying to whatever gods would listen that she wasn't too late.

Andinen coughed, gagging on the liquid she'd given him. She clutched him, starting to sob once more. "Please come back to me." She managed between desperate sobs. "Please come back." She started to sing, her voice raw and scratchy, but she didn't care. She sang the lullaby, rocking him back and forth.

He coughed again, sputtering, and his eyes drifted open. "Mama?" he murmured before grabbing her arm in a small hand and closing his eyes once more.

"Yes, baby. I'm here." She stared at him, not daring to hope that he was recovering. But yes. His breathing grew stronger. More regular. The color returned to his cheeks.

She clutched him to her chest, and she could feel his little heart beating against her body. Slow but strong. Consistent. She looked around the room. *They'll keep coming for him,* she realized. Vel was dead — killed by the thing possessing Andinen, but still dead. That should buy her some time.

Still holding Andinen, she stood and moved to the dresser where his clothes were kept. She grabbed a few simple outfits from the drawers, then left the nursery and walked to her own chambers. Then into her oversized closet. In the back, she found an aged satchel — a relic from before her life in Avalon — and stowed Andinen's clothing inside. She grabbed an equally ragged cloak from another hook and wrapped it around herself, pulling the hood up. Finally, she kicked off her slippers and pulled on a well-worn pair of walking boots. She almost fell doing so, refusing to relinquish her hold on Andinen, but she managed.

Her jewelry went into the satchel — wealthy trappings that she would no longer need, but that were still valuable. A necklace given to her by Andin when they married she fastened around her neck, but the rest of the finery found a place on the bottom of her bag.

She went to the kitchen next, stowing food and other supplies for a journey. She'd sell some of the jewelry once she left Avalon, but she wanted to be several days away before trying that. She'd head for Frostvein, or perhaps Halrisk.

They'll know we survived, she realized. They'd be able to count the bodies. *They won't leave us be if they think we're alive.*

Her eyes fell on the flickering fire of the kitchen's hearth. It would destroy almost every memory of her husband, but she knew what she had to do.

Mara slipped into attunement and called the fire from the hearth. Though her throat hurt, she could do this last thing. The flames streamed to her, and she shifted the timbre of her note, pushing. She spread it from the kitchen into the hallways, onto the tapestries lining the walls, to the rugs, to the papers in Andin's office — untouched even after all these years. It grew as she sang, pushing the fire to engulf more of the mansion.

The fire spread deeper into Andin's home, and she walked through the dining room with Andinen held in her arms, his head still resting on her shoulder. His breathing still steady. The flames had spread up the stairs, toward the dozens of unused bedrooms. Smoke billowed toward her, and she coughed, the song falling from her lips. She looked at the frozen bodies of the choirguard and the harmonizers, at the shattered corpse of Festin. The flames were melting the ice now, and it wouldn't be long till they consumed the bodies encased within. The house would likely collapse on them, further obfuscating her escape.

Mara opened the door and slipped out into the comforting cocoon of night. She pulled the cloak around her shoulders, hunching low and holding Andinen close. Her boots echoed on the cobbles in the silent darkness as she made for the city gates. She turned and looked at the manor one last time, watching plumes of smoke rising against the violet night sky before walking away from Mara Vosburg forever.

ABOUT THE AUTHOR

Alfred Smith is a father and rowing coach from Erie, Pennsylvania. He found himself telling stories from a young age, and then made the logical step into running Dungeons and Dragons games when he was only 9 years old. He has settled in Erie, Pennsylvania for the foreseeable future with his wife, Emily, his daughter, Hope, and their cat, Lord Squeaky. Alfred has run the Parsec SFF Short Story Contest since 2020. He has been published in *Deep Magic Ezine*, and several anthologies from Air and Nothingness Press.

YOU MIGHT ALSO ENJOY

The Alchemist Daughter
by Paul S. Moore

When a concoction of ethers channels a little of their magic properties to one location, inspiration springs to life.

Grey Mother Mountain
by Elyse Russell

When her village is destroyed, an elderly woman seeks help from the last remaining dragon to get revenge.

Songs of a Dead Forest
by Travis Wade Beaty

Old songs can bring new life.

Available in digital and trade paperback editions from
Water Dragon Publishing
waterdragonpublishing.com

www.ingramcontent.com/pod-product-compliance
Lightning Source LLC
Chambersburg PA
CBHW051303190726
48286CB00004B/1237